Country Compan[ions]

The Photo Competition

Written by Karen King

Illustrations by Rosemary Sharman

By courtesy of Hallmark Cards UK

MADCAP

Ed Hedgehog was reading the newspaper. 'There's a photo competition in here,' he told his friend, Tom Mouse. 'The most unusual photo wins a prize.'

'Why don't you enter?' asked Tom. Ed always took unusual photos, even when he didn't mean to!

'I think I will,' said Ed.

He fetched his camera from his bedroom and went out to take some photographs.

'I must find something really unusual to photograph if I want to win the prize,' Ed thought, looking around.

Then he spotted Kit Vole exercising in his garden.

'Now that'll make a good photo,' he thought.

Ed put his camera to his eye as Kit picked up a heavy dumbbell.

'Smile Kit!' he shouted.

'What?' gasped Kit. He was so startled he dropped the dumbbell on his foot – just as Ed took the photograph.

'Ow!' wailed Kit, hopping around, holding his foot.

'Sorry,' said Ed. 'I'm taking some photos for a competition.'

Kit didn't look too pleased so Ed thought he'd better go and find someone else to photograph.

As he walked along the street, Ed saw Sam Rabbit helping Madame Fleur carry some plants into her flower shop.

'Now, that would make a good photo,' Ed thought as Sam picked up a tall, very unusual-looking plant.

Ed put his camera to his eye. 'Smile Sam!' he shouted.

Sam turned around to smile, tripped over the step and dropped the plant just as Ed took his photograph.

'Ouch!' groaned Sam, rubbing his leg and glaring at Ed.

'Sorry,' said Ed. 'I'm taking some photos for a competition.'

Sam didn't look too pleased so Ed thought he'd better look for someone else to photograph.

A little while later, Ed saw Badger cleaning his car.

'That will make a good photo,' Ed thought as Badger sprayed the car roof with the hosepipe.

'Smile, Badger!' shouted Ed.

But when Badger turned to smile at Ed, he accidentally sprayed the hosepipe over Olly Owl, who was walking past!

'Aargh!' spluttered Olly. 'I'm drenched!'

'Oh dear, I am sorry,' apologised Badger.

Ed thought it was time he left!

He decided to have a break from taking photos and pop into the café for a snack.

In the café, Olivia was carrying a big plate of delicious-looking cakes over to one of the tables.

'That will make a good photo,' thought Ed, picking up his camera.

'Smile!' he shouted to Olivia.

Olivia was so startled she dropped the plate and the cakes went all over the floor.

'Now look what you've made me do!' she shouted crossly.

'Sorry!' said Ed. 'I was only taking your photograph.'

'Did you take some photos?' asked Tom when Ed returned home.

'Yes, but they all went wrong,' Ed told him, looking really disappointed. 'So I won't bother to enter the photo competition.'

He put his camera down and went out into the garden.

Tom looked at the camera and saw that there was only one more photo left. 'It's a shame not to finish the film,' he thought.

A little while later, Tom found Ed fast asleep in the wheelbarrow, snoring loudly. That gave him an idea.

He picked up a feather and held it over Ed's face. Then he let it go. The feather fluttered gently down. But when Ed snored he blew the feather back up again. Up and down it blew, up and down.

'Now, that'll make a good photo,' grinned Tom.

Tom took a photo of Ed blowing the feather back up in the air.

Then, he hurried to the chemist to have the film developed.

The photos were ready later that afternoon. Tom looked through them and had a good chuckle and decided to send the photos into the competition anyway.

So he put all the photos in a big envelope and put them in the post.

A few days later, Tom and Ed had a visit from a newspaper reporter. They had both won a prize in the photo competition. Ed was surprised to hear that he'd won first prize for the most unusual photo, after all. And Tom was even more surprised to hear that he'd won a consolation prize for the funniest photo!

Ed's prize was a new camera and Tom's prize was a pair of binoculars.

Ed was really pleased. 'Now I can practise taking more photos!' he smiled.

Other titles in this series

The Birthday Surprise (read and colour)
The Lost Wellingtons
The Picnic
The Summer Fayre

The Summer Fayre and **The Lost Wellingtons**
are also available as book and tape and as an audio tape
from MCI Children's Audio

First published in Great Britain by Madcap Books, André Deutsch Ltd, 76 Dean Street, London, W1V 5HA
André Deutsch is a subsidiary of VCI plc
www.vci.co.uk

Text and illustrations copyright © 1998 Madcap Books
Country Companions™ © Hallmark Cards UK

A catalogue record for this title is available from the British Library

ISBN 0 233 99229 4

Printed in the UK